For Milo
E.B.

For Helen Craig
D.P.

Text copyright © 1993 by Eileen Browne
Illustrations copyright © 1993 by David Parkins

First U.S. edition 1993
First published in Great Britain in 1993 by Walker Books Ltd., London.

Library of Congress Cataloging-in-Publication Data
Browne, Eileen.
No problem / Eileen Browne; illustrated by David Parkins.—1st U.S. ed.

Summary: Mouse's friends take turns putting together the pieces that
come in a box as a birthday present; but, only Shrew, who takes the
time to read the instructions, is able to build something that really works.

[1. Mice—Fiction. 2. Animals—Fiction. 3. Reading—Fiction.]
I. Parkins, David, ill. II. Title.
PZ7.B81995No 1993   92-53134
ISBN 1-56402-176-9 (book)
ISBN 1-56402-200-5 (book and kit)

10 9 8 7 6 5 4 3 2 1

Printed in Hong Kong

The artwork in this book is pen and watercolor.

Candlewick Press
2067 Massachusetts Avenue
Cambridge, Massachusetts 02140

No Problem

by
Eileen Browne

illustrated by
David Parkins

CONSTRUCTION KIT

To Mouse,
Put together the thing you see,
Then climb aboard and visit me!
Love from Rat

THIS WAY UP

CANDLEWICK PRESS
CAMBRIDGE, MASSACHUSETTS

One morning, Mouse was woken up
by a heavy CLONK! outside her front door.
Whatever's that? Mouse thought. She
hopped out of bed, opened the door, and
looked outside. In front of her was an
ENORMOUS package. It was wrapped in brown
paper and tied with string.
  CONSTRUCTION KIT was stamped on the
front and a pink card hung from the side.
It read,

  To Mouse,
  Put together the things you see,
  Then climb aboard and visit me!
  Love from Rat.

  "Oooooh!" squeaked Mouse.
    She nibbled through the string,
      peeled off the paper, and
        opened the package.

Inside was a mountain of bits and pieces—
just *waiting* to be put together.
  Mouse sniffed them and snuffled them.
She poked them and prodded them.
"I can put these together," she said.
"NO problem."

To Mouse,
Put together the things you see,
Then climb aboard and visit me!
  Love from Rat

She was in such a hurry to begin that she *forgot* to look for the instructions.

Mouse got to work. She joined pipes here and attached wheels there. She twisted and turned things. She fiddled and twiddled things. She bolted bolts and tightened nuts.

Then she stepped back to see what she'd made.

"Gosh!" said Mouse. "What *can* it be?
It's a little like a bike . . . but it isn't a bike.
I think I'll call it a Biker-Riker."
    She climbed on, started the engine, and set off to see Rat.

The Biker-Riker was very jumpy and very wobbly.   It jumped

from wheel to wheel and kept popping "wheelies" by mistake.

"Ooooh!" cried Mouse, hanging on tight. "Maybe I didn't put it together right."

She was tottering along on one wheel, when she met Badger.

"Well, hello there, Mouse," growled Badger, peering over the top of her glasses. "What is that very peculiar *thing* you're riding?"

"It's a Biker-Riker," squeaked Mouse. "A present from Rat. I put it together, but I don't think it's right. It's very jumpy and very wobbly."

"Do you have the instructions?" asked Badger.

"No," said Mouse. "Can you help?"

Badger polished her glasses and blinked at the Biker-Riker. "Well now," she mumbled. "Let's see. Hmmmmmm."

Then she looked up and said, "I can fix this. NO problem."

Badger unscrewed the screws and unbolted the bolts. She shifted and shoved things. She changed and rearranged things. She reset the pipes and the wheels.

Then she stepped back to see what she'd made.

"Ahhh," said Badger. "What *can* it be? It's a little like a car . . . but it isn't a car. I think I'll call it a Jaloppy-Doppy."

"Come on," said Mouse. "Let's go to Rat's."

Mouse and Badger climbed into the Jaloppy-Doppy and set off to see Rat.

The Jaloppy-Doppy was very bumpy and very rattly,

and not at all comfortable.

"May-be," said Badger, bouncing up and down, "I did-n't put it to-ge-ther ri-ght."

They were juddering along a riverbank, when they met Otter.

"Hey!" Otter grinned. "What the heck is that?"

"It's a Jaloppy-Doppy," snorted Badger. "Rat sent it to Mouse. I put it together, but I don't think it's right. It's very bumpy and very rattly."

"Got the instructions?" asked Otter.

"Sadly, no," said Badger. "Can you help?"

Otter dived into the Jaloppy-Doppy and rolled out again. She climbed up the front and slid down the back.

"I can fix this," said Otter. "NO problem."

She squeezed underneath and unbolted the bolts. She flipped things and flopped things. She switched things and swapped things. She moved all the wheels and she rebuilt the pipes.

Then she stepped back to see what she'd made.

"Wow!" barked Otter. "What *can* it be? It's a little like a
boat . . . but it isn't a boat. I'm gonna call it a Boater-Roater."
"Come on," said Mouse and Badger. "Let's go to Rat's."
Mouse, Badger, and Otter pushed the Boater-Roater onto
the river. They jumped in and set off to see Rat.

The Boater-Roater kept rocking and rolling,

and letting in lots of water.

"Geeeeee," said Otter, swaying to and fro. "Mayb*eeeee* I didn't put it tog*eeeee*ther r*iiiiii*ght."

They were sailing around a bend, when they met Shrew.

"Hi!" piped Shrew. "What's that?"

"It's a Boater-Roater," said Otter. "Rat sent it to Mouse. I put it together, but I don't think it's right. It keeps rocking and rolling."

"Do you have the instructions?" asked Shrew.

"No," said Otter. "Can you help?"

Shrew jumped into the Boater-Roater and scampered all over it. She peeped into corners, peered through pipes, and peeked around poles. Then . . . she found something.

"YES!" said Shrew. "I can fix this. NO problem."

They pulled the Boater-Roater onto the riverbank.

Shrew didn't

She *completely dismantled* the Boater-Roater.

And peering down

"Pass me this!"
she ordered Mouse.

"Pass me that!"
she snapped at Badger.

"Give me those!"
she said to Otter.

switch things,   or swap things,   or flip things,   or flop things.

at a sheet of paper, she laid all the pieces in rows on the grass.

Then piece by piece and nut by bolt, she built a wonderful . . .

CONSTRUCTION KIT
(How to Put it Together?)

AIRPLANE!

"How did you do it?" asked Mouse, Badger, and Otter.

"Easy!" laughed Shrew. "I followed the instructions!"
And she waved a sheet of paper that said,

CONSTRUCTION KIT.

HOW TO PUT IT TOGETHER!

"Well, I'll be!" said the others. "Come on, let's go to Rat's."

So Mouse, Badger, Otter, and Shrew climbed into the airplane and set off to see Rat.

They raced across the grass and rose into the air.

"*Yoo-reeka!*" squeaked Mouse.

"*Yowler-rowler!*" growled Badger.

"*Bonanza!*" barked Otter.

"*Yazoo!*" piped Shrew.

The airplane didn't jump or wobble,
or bump or rattle, or rock or roll. It just flew
smoothly through the sky all the way to Rat's.

They landed the plane and climbed out.

"Look!" said Mouse. "There are balloons on Rat's door. She must be having a party."

The door swung open and out jumped Rat.

"HAPPY BIRTHDAY, MOUSE!" said Rat.

"Happy birthday," said Badger and Otter and Shrew. "Did you forget? It's your birthday! We're having a party."

"My birthday?" said Mouse. "Well, I never!"

"I see you got the airplane," said Rat. "Did you have any trouble putting it together?"

Mouse winked at Badger. Otter winked at Shrew.
"NO problem," they said.